Lulu's First Day

by Anna McQuinn

Illustrated by Rosalind Beardshaw

Alanna Max

Tomorrow is a big day for Lulu.
She is starting pre-school!

It will be a bit like her story time group at the library, but Lulu will stay by herself.

Lulu visited the school last month,
so she knows what to expect.

Nana gave Lulu a new bag for school.
Tayo gave her a water bottle.

Lulu wants to wear her party dress to school. Mummy says maybe not.

So Lulu chooses her pink, jumping leggings and her sunny, yellow top.

Lulu puts everything on her chair ready for the morning.

She has packed her bag with all her things
and extra clothes... just in case.

Everyone gets up super early.

Lulu puts Dinah in her bag.
Now she's ready. Time for photos!

Miss Suzan welcomes everyone.
She shows Lulu where to put Dinah
and the rest of her things.

Mummy sits with the other
grown-ups for a little while.

Lulu can choose what to do first.

Julie is reading.
Lulu decides to read too.

The story gives Lulu an idea.

Lulu and Julie run to the dress-up box.
Now they are superheroes!

Mummy said goodbye and went home.
She will be back later. Lulu hugs Dinah
and feels better.

Soon it is snack time. Everyone sits to eat.

After snack time, Lulu and Julie
build a huge castle .

Mo and Tien join in.

Next it's circle time. Lulu already knows lots of the songs. Then they sing a goodbye song.

Mummy is waiting outside.
It is time to go home already!

Mummy gives Lulu a big hug.
They say good bye to
Miss Suzan and Julie.

Lulu and Mummy have a snack at home.
Pre-school is fun... but exhausting.

Shh! Lulu has fallen asleep!

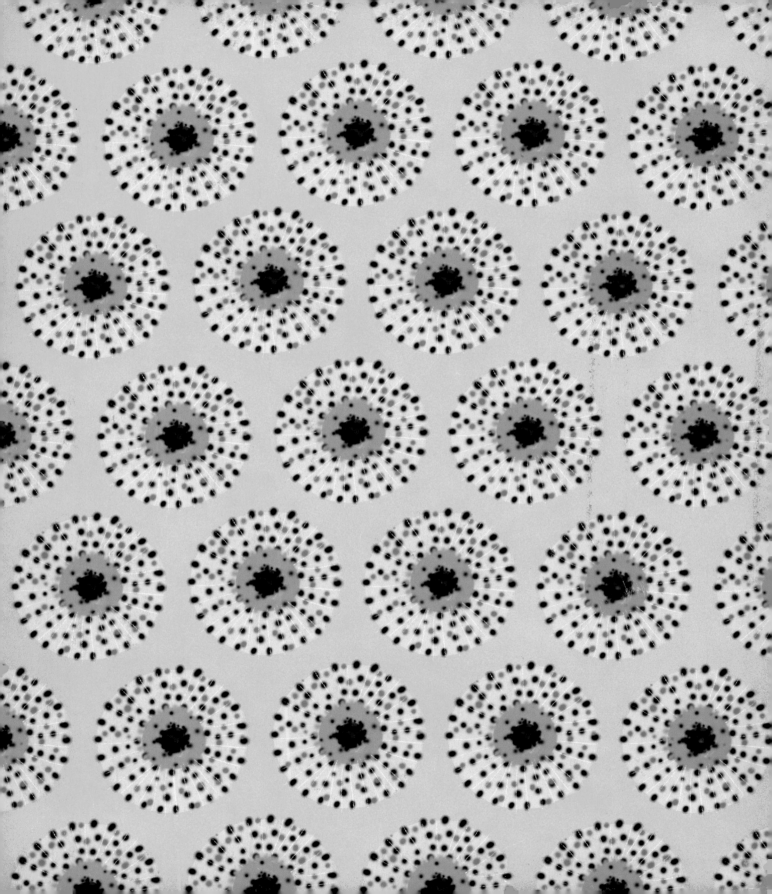